Mt. Lebanon Public Library
16 Castle Shannon Boulevard
Pittsburgh, PA 15228-2252
412 531-1912
www.einpgh.org/ein/net/mtleb

DISCARDED BY
MT LEBANON LIBRARY

MORGY'S MUSICAL SUMMER

MORGY'S MUSICAL SUMMER

by Maggie Lewis

Illustrated by Michael Chesworth

Houghton Mifflin Company
Boston 2008

MAY 08 2008
Lewis

Mt. Lebanon Public Library
Children's Library

Text copyright © 2008 by Maggie Lewis
Illustrations copyright © 2008 by Michael Chesworth

All rights reserved. For information about permission to reproduce selections from this book, write to Permissions, Houghton Mifflin Company, 215 Park Avenue South, New York, New York 10003.

www.houghtonmifflinbooks.com

The text of this book is set in 12.5-point Cheltenham.

Library of Congress Cataloging-in-Publication Data

Lewis, Maggie.
Morgy's musical summer / written by Maggie Lewis ; illustrated by Michael Chesworth.
p. cm.
Summary: To encourage his talent for playing the trumpet, Morgy is sent to a music camp over the summer, where he has the displeasure of meeting Damian, an advanced student who likes to tease "promising beginners."
ISBN-13: 978-0-618-77707-5
[1. Music camps—Fiction. 2. Camps—Fiction. 3. Musicians—Fiction.] I. Chesworth, Michael, ill. II. Title.
PZ7.L58726Ms 2008
[Fic]—dc22
2007025780

Manufactured in the United States of America
VB 10 9 8 7 6 5 4 3 2 1

For Morgan Lewis and Owen Thomas

With thanks to Nathan Cohen, William Mix,
and Kenyon Wilson

CONTENTS

ONE
Outlook, Look Out

To: Campers and Parents
Re: Outlook Music Camp Rules and Regulations

Rules for Campers:
Number one: Have fun.
Number two: Play true.
Number three: Respect—the staff, camp rules, other campers, instruments, yourself.

Rules for Parents:
One phone call.
Please, no food packages. We serve wholesome meals and snacks and do not wish to attract extra bears.
Label everything with first and last names. Packing list follows.

Looking forward to a musical summer, I remain, yours sincerely,

Colonel Hiram Profundo,
retired, U.S. Air Force

Dear Keith,
I have ten pairs of underpants with my name on them. From now on I can't e-mail you. I'll write and tell you what cabin I'm in as soon as I know. Send me letters! Postcards! Anything!

Gulp,
Morgy

Leaving for camp took all day. Mom counted everything one more time, a couple of times. We still had to find a soap dish, a beach towel, and sun lotion. I even wrote my name on the soap. Dad gave me his portable alarm clock from college.

"It seems like a long way to go to get better at the trumpet," I said. Dad said it wasn't just the trumpet, it was camp and I'd love it. Colonel Profundo, a famous band leader, lived in our town, Puckett Corner, Massachusetts. In the summers, he ran Outlook Music Camp in Maine. He was letting me and my friend Byron Noonan come for free because he thought we were promising beginners.

Mom said that was so generous of him. This way, the Noonans could still afford to send Byron to hockey camp. I was going, too. We were going to car pool. "You'll be back home before you know it—in time for hockey camp!" said Mom, to cheer me up. Byron goes to hockey camp every summer. Last year, Mom lost the sign-up sheet so I couldn't go. This year, she remembered. But three weeks of sleep-away music camp seemed kind of long to me. And besides, I only wanted to worry about one camp at a time.

Mom found another washcloth. She wrapped the alarm clock in it and buckled my trunk. She and Dad carried it out and put it in the back of our car. Dante, my greyhound, got excited. He loves the car. He wasn't coming, though. Pancake, my cat, brushed against me and ran upstairs. I put my hand on Dante's forehead. "I'll be back." He wiggled his eyebrows.

"You're supposed to have four washcloths," said Mom, and kissed me. She was staying home with my twin sisters, Phoebe and Penelope, plus Dante and Pancake. Dad was driving me up to Outlook. "I'd give you Phoebe's giraffe bath mitt, but she would miss it."

"I'll be fine," I said. When I moved to Puckett Corner I learned that it's a good idea not to show up in a new place with anything extra doofy for people to laugh at.

"Ppplll!" Penelope staggered toward me with her tongue out. She'd just learned to walk, but she could make that noise before she could sit up. "Moo," said Phoebe, sitting on the floor and trying to grab me. I kissed them on the tops of their heads. They drool.

Mom waved. Dante stood with her. He kept his ears up and pointed his nose after us. We had to go back for my trumpet. He was so happy, he jumped around in a circle. "Sorry, boy," I said. He kept his ears up and watched us, in case it was a game.

I waved till we got to the end of the street. At Mack's Corner Spa, Mack and Tom, Byron's big brother, were bringing in a big stack of tomorrow's funny papers. In the park where five roads come together, seven Hagopian cousins and brothers and sisters were in the sandbox and on the swings, with just Clara Hagopian's father. Usually their grandmother took them to the park, but she was driving Clara to camp. Clara plays flute better than a promising beginner.

We got on the turnpike, then another highway.

Maybe even another one. I fell asleep. I woke up going uphill on a thin gray road. Grass and white flowers whipped by, plus motels, water-skiing places, and pine trees. Then a white, arrow-shaped sign that said "Outlook" flew past us, pointing up a shady road.

"Whoa," I said.

"Oops-a-daisy," Dad said, putting on the brakes. "Good thing you woke up. We might have driven all the way to Canada." I wondered if we really were that far away, if I really was that promising, and if people who could play trumpet better than you got as mad at you as people who can play hockey better. Also, what did Colonel Profundo mean by extra bears? We parked in a field. On one side of the road, at the very top of the hill, was a white house. It had a tower. In front of it was a cannon. On the other side of the road, cabins and a lake. The cannon was pointed at us.

"That must be the Outlook. It dates back to the Revolutionary War. They have concerts here, too," said Dad. "I guess we have to carry your trunk down to one of those cabins." He opened the back of the station wagon. A chilly breeze blew in. The cozy car smell of Dante and the girls' teething crackers blew away.

OUTLOOK

Colonel Profundo came across the road in a musical note T-shirt that I had ten of. He has a sharp nose and white hair with a very straight part. He grabbed Dad's hand, and Dad thanked him for letting me come. Colonel Profundo said nonsense, Byron and I did his heart good. He looked at his clipboard. I was in Mozart. He told Dad to back up and take a left at a dirt road. It went behind the cabins. Mozart was the fourth one down. We could unload my trunk there. "Concert's at five," he said.

The cabins were small, with porches and signs over their doors. We went by Bach, Beethoven, and Brahms. Mozart, a little out of line, was right where the dirt road went into the woods. It smelled like pine trees and mothballs inside. "Great!" said Dad. Then he hit his head on a rafter. He told me to take a bottom bunk. "Easier to make, so you'll pass inspections." He said all camps had inspections; otherwise people hid snacks under their beds and raccoons got in, looking for them. "But they tell you it's bears so you'll take them seriously," he said.

That was good news. "What about the one phone call?" I said. But another dad came in with a trunk and a cello case, crashed into a bunk, and backed out. Then a mother came in and opened a trunk. She unfolded a red comforter with a serious gray Beethoven face on it. She put on red pillowcases and folded down matching sheets with lines and musical notes in black.

"Dah-dah-dah dahhhh," said Dad. "It's the beginning of Beethoven's fifth symphony."

My sheets had dancing Snoopys on them. We got them in California, when I was little, at a yard sale. "Mom sent these because it doesn't matter what happens to them," said Dad, in case the Beethoven kid made fun of me later. Right then, I didn't care. I was homesick for California and Puckett Corner at the same time.

When the kid and his mom left, Dad told me to put on my camp uniform. I didn't think you were supposed to just undress in the middle of Mozart, but he was already pulling off my T-shirt. "Just like when my dad joined the army. Do you remember Grumpapa's story about mailing his clothes home because he knew he wouldn't need them till the war was over?" Then he scruffed up my hair. I thought he would say, "Don't worry, it's not a war," but a bugle blew.

"Whoops!" A tall redheaded kid ran in while I was in my underpants with MORGY MACDOUGAL-

MACDUFF markered on the waistband. "It's time for the concert. I'm Gus, and I'll be your son's counselor." He shook hands with Dad, got a saxophone out of a case, ducked to miss the rafter, and ran up the hill, putting a strap around his neck.

We walked up through the grass. White flowers knocked us on the knees. The kid with the Beethoven comforter, his mom, and his brothers walked behind us. We crossed the road to the white house. I didn't hold Dad's hand. I was going into fifth grade in the fall. "Do you think Dante will get enough walks?" I said. Dad said Phoebe and Penelope love going out in the stroller with him. Mom would take him on all her errands, probably. Dad promised to take him out for a longer time after dinner, too, "if he's not too tired." He smiled, to get me to smile.

On the porch of the white house, counselors were tuning their instruments. Parents and kids stood on the grass. I was going to ask Dad to let Pancake sleep in his and Mom's bed, but the colonel said, "We'll start with a Mozart horn concerto, play the march from Bizet's *Carmen*, a little Sousa march, and then a song I dearly love." They played loud, together, and fast, just the opposite of the Puckett Corner Elementary School band. You could feel the

drums in your stomach. The song he dearly loved was “The Star-Spangled Banner.” Dad took off his baseball cap and put it over his heart. Before you knew it—*bup-pa, bwaaah!*—they were finished.

The counselors bowed. Everyone clapped. Then they all backed up. Some kids put their fingers in their ears. The colonel lit a match. “Summer has begun,” he said.

Puh-BOOM! went the cannon. It rolled back on its wheels and sent a puff of smoke toward the lake. A dog barked and a little girl started to cry. *Puh-boom,* echoed the echo. “Parents, if you please,” said the colonel, and bowed. The Beethoven mom handed out water bottles with black and white straps marked like a piano keyboard to her three sons. Dad gave me a big hug. “I’ll write every day,” he said. Over his shoulder I saw Clara Hagopian kiss her grandmother on the cheek.

I stood on a boulder and watched our car, one of the smallest, wait for its turn to drive away. It took so long, I could have gotten back in. I hoped Mom wouldn’t let go of Dante’s leash like she did once last winter. It wasn’t her fault, but he could run really fast and he didn’t know about traffic. Our car climbed down the gray road and disappeared around a piney corner.

Then Byron was standing next to me on the rock. "Look," he said. "It's the horn player from Boston Baked Brass." She was on the porch of the white house with the other counselors, holding her curvy French horn. Last time we saw her, she was in our cafeteria at school, with her curly red hair covering the back of her chair like Rapunzel's would if she did school assemblies, and Byron was standing up and applauding. Now she had a thick braid sticking out the back of her Outlook baseball cap. "Excellent," Byron said.

"Where's your van?" I said.

"Savanna and Mike brought me. Savanna's driving Mike to a smokejumper training camp." My aunt Savanna married Byron's uncle Mike over spring vacation.

I saw our car driving out of the pines, way down by the water-ski place. Then it went around the edge of the lake and disappeared. If I were Dante, I could still run and catch up. Mr. Profundo, our trumpet teacher from school, went by carrying a big box of strawberries. "Hey, guys. Gramps told me you were coming. I hope you're ready to work!"

Back in Mozart we told our names and instruments. Nathan played the cello. So did Jonathan.

Two cellos in a cabin could make it pretty crowded, Gus, the counselor, said, but Nathan and Jonathan were working on a duet. There was a violinist named John. Brendan had a twin but just by himself played drums, piano, and clarinet. Everyone's shorts were faded. They came every summer. They all started playing their instruments in kindergarten or first grade. Johan, with the Beethoven comforter, started playing the flute in fourth grade, like me with the trumpet. But that was just for a break from piano lessons. His dad started teaching him piano when he was three. His dad played the piano for a living. I was the only promising beginner.

They blew a bugle for dinner, which was in the white house with the tower. We had spaghetti that was too sticky to go down my throat. My aunt Savanna told me that when she went to camp, on an island full of bears and girls who were serious about volleyball, she didn't want to eat for a week. I must not have been homesick, because I was hungry. But I must have been something, because I was telling Savanna stories to myself. There are a lot of Savanna stories. You can get tired of them.

Everyone sat with their cabins. Byron was in the corner by the stone fireplace. Across the room I saw Clara looking serious between two girls who were talking at once and laughing. Brendan, at our table, and his twin, Trevor, at the next table, got the rims of their water glasses wet and ran their fingers around them.

"Benjamin Franklin had an instrument made out of those," I said. A girl named Maria put that in a report last year in Mr. Hansom's class. "Duh," said Johan. *SQUEEEE*, went the glasses.

Colonel Profundo tapped his glass with a fork, and they stopped. "Good evening, musicians," he said, "and I do not use the term lightly. Music is tough, practicing is long, scales are hard, and wrong notes are easy, as you all know. What you might forget is that you are each here because you have a gift. Whether you're a promising beginner or an advanced student getting ready for a competition, we are here to help you give your gift. Because no matter what anyone tells you, there's always a need for a snappy tune, well played. Sad to say, there might not always be an Outlook Music Camp. In fact, because of finances, we may be closing after this session." People started talking. "So, stay focused, boys and girls, and practice. And if it comes to that and they take that Outlook sign down, you keep playing."

One of the girls next to Clara started to cry.

Colonel Profundo sat down and a lady with gray hair stood up and said, "Just a few more announcements," but everyone was making too much noise about camp closing. "Now, now, we still have three weeks. Meanwhile!" They quieted down. "Remember that the road that goes through camp is not part of camp. It has been here longer than we have, and everyone drives too fast, so do look both ways when you cross. Outlook sweatshirts are ready and are under the piano. Check the bulletin board for lesson times. And our grandson Hank made strawberry shortcake." Chairs scooted out all over the room.

The shortcake was in big pieces, with whipped cream. Easy to swallow. I thought I would be OK. I mean, not too homesick. After dinner, Byron and I waited for the big kids to get out of the way so we could see the bulletin board. "We both have Ms. Rapontin," said Byron. "I wonder if that's her? I heard some kid call her Veronica. Veronica Rapontin?"

"Yes," said a voice. It was her, the French horn player. I introduced us.

"So you're Morgy," she said. "I've heard about you. Well, time for campfire. Byron, welcome," she said. Byron's hand came out of the cuff of his new sweatshirt and she shook it. Then she hustled off.

"You're blushing," said Byron.

"No, you are," I said.

Campfire was across the road and down a long path under pine trees. They were so thick it was almost dark under them. It was like a race getting there. A kid pushed Byron. I tripped on a tree root. Someone put a hand on my shoulder. I shook it off.

"Um, hey?" It was Clara.

"Sorry," I said. She told us the person who got to the campfire first got to light the fire. The last person there had to play a solo on any instrument the colonel chose. So we hurried, too. We came to a beach and sat on a log.

A girl with skinny legs and raggedy blond hair, the one who cried when the cannon went off, lit the fire. A tall kid with long brown hair and a ripped sport coat instead of an Outlook sweatshirt slouched out of the woods. The colonel handed him a saxophone. The kid raised one eyebrow and made a long, twisty tune come out of it. Clara said it was an oboe part from *The Nutcracker Suite,* and he was playing it on the saxophone to be sassy. But the colonel, and everyone, clapped. "No more being last on purpose, Damian," he said, and then we sang the camp song:

We are the Outlook campers,
Not a bad note in the bunch.
We play the tunes from dawn to dusk
And never miss our lunch.
Outlook, Outlook, Outlook, look out!
Practice, practice, each day starts with a shout!

There are a lot of verses, and you always get to shout the word "shout." We also sang songs about combing your hair with a frying pan; Charlie, who can't get off the train; and the cowboy who loved you so true. Then a sad one. It's about a blackbird. "Bye-bye, blackbird," some counselors sang, in harmony, "blackbird, bye-bye." It made me think of Dante. He's black. He has two white toes, and he smiles. I cried, but it was dark.

Back in Mozart, after we got our pajamas on and went to the bathroom in the wash house, Gus turned off the light bulb. I should have told Dad to let Pancake sleep in his and Mom's bed. He just wants to lie on your feet for a while, then he gets up and walks around on the window seat or goes down to the kitchen to finish his kibbles. My feet felt different, not being squashed by a fluffy orange cat. It was so dark, I almost didn't know if my eyes were open or closed. Then I saw a little light off to the left of my bed. I reached out to see if it was Dad's alarm clock, but it was farther away. I thought it was a firefly in the field. I watched for it to flicker, but I fell asleep.

TWO
Pine Siskin

Dear Morgy,

Look what I found as soon as you and Dad left! Two more washcloths! Here's a glider to play with. I'm excited for you, Puppy Dog. Write me all about your cabin and new friends. I'm so proud, and your uniform is very, very cute.

Love,

Mom

Then there were three smiley faces and one frowny face that said "Missing Morgy."

Dear Morgy,

I get to use the fax machine. How's camp? I'm

doing "Soccer X-perience." We run in the mountains!! I am goalie! For once! Raul is playing center. Wahoo!

Keith

I was embarrassed to get a FedEx package with two ladybug washcloths in it. But Damian, the slouchy guy who played the saxophone solo, got a pair of Big Bird slippers. In one slipper was a sheet of music. Even rolled up, it looked like hard music. It was all eighth and sixteenth notes, tied together, with writing and marks over them, and no blank spaces where you could put your instrument on your knee and let someone else play. "What are you looking at?" Damian said. I put the washcloths in my shorts pocket and didn't answer.

Byron got an envelope from his big brother, Tom, with no letter but a pack of gum in it. The mailboxes were behind the grand piano in the Outlook. Upstairs were all the lesson rooms. The stairs were a kind of spiral with corners. Kids ran up and down them with instruments or waited on benches built into the corners. All the big wood doors were closed. Kids were tuning up. Strings plinked. Clarinets and flutes went up, *tootle oot?* as if they were asking a question, and down, *tootle*

oot! as if they were mad. A tuba played a scale. A person behind a closed door sang a scale too loud.

Brroot, taroot! Right behind us, Ms. Rapontin was testing a trumpet. "I guess that works, then," she said when we jumped. "Do you know 'Pop! Goes the Weasel'? I'll teach it to you for the game."

Her classroom was all the way at the top. We blew her an A. We played what we knew, "God Rest Ye Merry, Gentlemen" and "Ode to Joy." She reminded us to keep our mouths tight and not blow out our cheeks. She taught us a scale. She showed us the music to "Pop! Goes the Weasel" and asked if we could read it. We couldn't. Well, I could, a little.

"You really are promising beginners," she said. "Of course, I wouldn't expect anything less from Hank Profundo." She put her trumpet to her lips and played "Pop! Goes the Weasel." She got it to sound surprising. Maybe because she twinkled her eyes at us while she played it. Byron forgot to play when it was our turn. We had to start over. She checked Byron's trumpet.

I sat down on the window seat. It must have been the top window of The Outlook. You could see all the way across the lake to some low mountains. A trail went up between two peaks. I could even see a line of people walking up the trail under the pine trees. Then Byron finally blew an A, so I had to pay attention again. By the time the bugle blew at the end of the hour, we almost had the first line, "Round and round the mulberry bush." Then she stayed over to teach us the end, "Pop! goes the weasel!" because we'd need to know it for the game.

"Her eyes are the same color as the trumpet," said Byron on the way downstairs.

"Wait, green?" I said.

"I mean the sparkles, duh. Golden, like the trumpet."

I thought of calling her "your girlfriend," because he said that to me, about Clara, for no good reason, in fourth grade. But I was glad I didn't because just then, right behind us, Ms. Rapontin yelled, "Time for musical chairs!" and ran past us. We helped her set up folding chairs on the porch. Colonel Profundo opened the windows and sat down at the piano. "You have to run all the way around the house while the music plays," he said. "When it stops, sit down in a chair. The one who doesn't get a chair stays on the porch and plays along with me. The rest get up and run around the house again. We play till everyone's playing music. The last one running around the house wins. Please don't cut through Mrs. Profundo's roses."

Ms. Rapontin conducted. We had to run uphill around the roses, and down the other side around the boulder. The first time, Damian ran through Mrs. Profundo's roses. His sport jacket caught on a thorn, so he was last and had to stay on the porch and play. Next time, Johan with the flute from my cabin was last. Next time around, just as I was about to run up the porch steps, Clara sat in the last chair. She joined us the next round.

"Faster, *presto!*" said Ms. Rapontin when only Byron and a tall girl with braids were left running. The other kids—Damian, Johan, and Clara, plus Gerry Ann, who did blow her cheeks out when she played her trombone, Trevor or his twin, Brendan, on drums, another kid with just a snare drum, and about fourteen violinists—ripped through it. I just played the beginning and end and I had to hurry. Byron got the last chair. He got up and bowed for the girl with the braids to sit and play "Pop! Goes the Weasel" on her tuba. Colonel Profundo came out on the porch, held up Byron's arm, and said, "Winner and still champ! I like this guy. Could have used you in the Air Force Band, any number of times!" Byron gulped for air and looked happy. Ms. Rapontin was smiling at him.

Then we had snacks. Hank Profundo brought a jumbo box of saltines out the kitchen door. We got to pump our own glasses of water from a pump. We sat on the boulder, which was warm, and ate and drank. Then it was time for musical groups. Hank read names. We lined up. Counselors took us to different places to practice, where we wouldn't hear each other. Somewhere there was a barn, but Clara, Byron, and I got sent down to the lake with some other kids for marching band with a tall guy with a ponytail in bike shorts.

"We're going to work on the marching part today, and do just the beginning of the song," he said. "If you already know it, be patient." The song was "Yankee Doodle." We tried the first few notes. Byron did a big loud *broot!* at exactly the wrong time. Some girls laughed. Pete, the kid with the snare drum, turned around to look at him and said something to Brendan.

"Did you see that?" Byron said when the flutes were playing by themselves.

"Shh!" said Gerry Ann, and went *broo-too-toot-*

toot at the right time on trombone. She was good, even with her cheeks puffed out.

We practiced marching around in the gray sand by the lake. It was getting warmer. A Jet Ski buzzed by, far away. I thought I could still see the trail going up the crack between the mountains, and even the line of people marching back down. I told Byron. "Maybe it's another camp," he said, standing still to look. Everyone marched into us.

"Watch me," said Clara, and showed us how to turn.

"Shhh!" said Gerry Ann.

"The promising beginners are weird," said Pete, and the girl with a fife said, "Shh, he just looked at you." I looked at the band leader just in time to play. Byron looked across the lake again, then went *Braaa!* at the wrong time again and we had to start over.

The band leader told everyone to take a rest. Then he came over to me and Byron.

"You boys have played in a band before, haven't you?"

"We have!" said Byron.

"We didn't march, though," I said.

"Well, keep trying." Marching was hard. You had to stand up really straight, bend your knees at the same time as everyone else, and hold your instrument either right up by your mouth or in front of you, ready to play. Clara could do it and still look normal. I kept poking my knee up at the wrong time. Byron put his arm down so hard it made a rude noise. Pete and Brendan laughed. Byron didn't pay any attention. Then it was time to play. I forgot and blew my cheeks out. This was harder than hockey.

Byron was frowning and playing. His cheeks weren't blowing out, but he was playing a lot of wrong notes. The other trumpeters moved away from us. But the band leader came over, smiling. "Everyone else go to lunch. Byron—is that your name?—ask your teacher for some help with the tune. You've got a good sound there. Nice lungs. Are you Morgy? Tomorrow, when we have groups, you go to junior orchestra instead, OK?"

"OK," I said. I guessed I was kicked out of marching band. I thought Byron always did better, probably because if you were good at a sport it helped you with everything. Lungs, anyway.

Clara waited for us at lunch. You didn't have to sit with your cabin. You picked whatever sandwich you wanted, an apple, milk, and a huge cookie.

"They don't believe in potato chips," said Clara.

"You'll do great in band," she told Byron. I saw the little blond girl who had lit the campfire.

"Is she in junior orchestra?" I said.

"No," said Clara, "she takes special piano lessons. She was on *Good Morning America*." Damian sat down with us.

"Hi, Clara," he said.

"Hi, Damian. How's oboe?" said Clara.

"Good. Are you in my quartet?"

"She's in band," said Byron.

"In the morning," said Damian. "After dinner, we're all in quartets—those of us who can read music." He laughed and walked away.

"Like I could be in his quartet," said Clara, and blushed. Byron frowned. One eyebrow up, the other down. He looked at me in a "This goes on for three weeks?" way. That was what I was thinking.

At quiet time you could write a letter or find a practice cabin in the woods. I didn't have anything to practice.

Dear Mom,
Thanks for the washcloths. Mozart gets the first showers, the water is cold, and there is a frog in the bath house. We had oatmeal for breakfast, blah!

How are Dante and Pancake? How are the girls? I wish I were there. I have to be in junior orchestra.

Love,

Morgy

I drew a frowny face.

After quiet time, we had sports. Mozart, Bach, and Beethoven did canoeing. Gus showed us how. I was the rudderer, the guy in back who steers. Byron paddled. After we followed Gus around the island, we could go where we wanted. The water was brown, but you could see straight through to the sticks, leaves, and pebbles on the bottom. A dragonfly kept up with us. There was a hot pine smell. But I felt even worse than I did in third grade when the hockey coach told me to practice with the seven-and-unders. I knew I couldn't play hockey, but I thought I was good at trumpet.

"Ms. Rapontin likes you best," Byron said.

"No."

"Yes. You could read the notes."

I felt better. I said, "I'm the one in junior orchestra, remember?"

"But with Ms. Rapontin," he said, and frowned.

The water was bubbling under the canoe. We were all going around the island. I said it was like the island by the riverboat ride at Disneyland, only real, but Byron didn't answer. I didn't know if he hadn't heard me or if he was mad that I got to be with Ms. Rapontin. On the way back, I said, "You could mess up on marching, too, if you want to be in junior orchestra."

That didn't cheer him up. "Huh," he said. He didn't think so, I guess.

Pete and Damian's canoe came up behind us. "No one could mess up like that on purpose," said Pete.

"For your information," said Damian, "Junior Orchestra is for advanced music students. It's only called that because there's a Senior Orchestra for the visiting musicians and some of the better counselors. You didn't get in by messing up. If you didn't audition, you must have been invited. I don't know why. But it is an excellent place for a trumpet to sit still and be quiet. See if you can do that, promising beginner."

I felt even worse, especially since that was what I was thinking. The marching band would be better off without my bad notes and worse marching. But Byron yelled, "See about your shorts! They're inside out!"

Damian actually checked, and they actually were. A brown head went by in the water. "What is that?"

said Byron, too loud. It ducked under.

"An otter," said Gus, paddling toward the dock. "You boys saw the first otter of the summer. That's excellent. Write it on the white board at tea."

At tea—graham crackers, with more water—I wrote "Morgy and Byron, otter," under "Clara and Gerry Ann, lady slipper," and "Damian, pine siskin."

"What's a pine siskin?" I said.

"Damian," said Byron, "is a pine siskin."

THREE
The Dork Orchestra

Keith,

Goalie! Excellent!! This is a postcard of Outlook. We eat dinner and breakfast in the white house, also we have a lesson in the tower, with a cool teacher. But I have to be in the dork orchestra. Fax me again, that was cool and excellent.

Morgy

Morgy,

Here are some stickers you're probably too old for. Do they have maple syrup? Try some on the oatmeal.

More later,

Dad

While Ms. Rapontin helped Byron with "Yankee Doodle" in our next lesson, I noticed a fire over on the other side of the lake, past where I'd seen the people marching uphill. Maybe that was the light I saw that first night. I would have told Byron, but he was watching Ms. Rapontin's hand on her trumpet, with his mouth open. When it was his turn, he played really loud and sat up straight. He got a lot of notes wrong, but he looked happy, even when Ms. Rapontin made him do it over. Then it was my turn. I just had to play some notes, not a whole song. They were part of something the junior orchestra would play called "Concerto Fabuloso."

"If you can just learn these measures this morning," said Ms. Rapontin, "junior orchestra will go smoother." She said measures are how music is divided up. Each one has the same amount of beats in it. They have lines between them on the page. She also taught me a G-sharp, which you have to play with two fingers on valves, instead of a plain old G with no fingers. Then she taught us "The monkey thought 'twas all in fun," so now we knew the whole first verse of "Pop! Goes the Weasel."

Not that Byron had to play it. That day, there was a much bigger group of kids on the front

porch, because the flute choir got finished with their practice early. They all played really fast, but Byron was still the last, fastest one. My hand got so sweaty, my fingers slipped off the valves. I wished I could run like that. The colonel had us pick up the pace for the last lap—Byron versus Pete, who was much older. Byron ran around the corner, but he didn't come back around the other

side of the house. I wondered if he fell down. Maybe he was hurt. Maybe he got sick of it and left. Then there he was on top of the boulder. He had climbed it. He ran down the front of it instead of staying between it and the house, and he still beat Pete. The colonel applauded. Pete sat down next to Brendan's twin brother, Trevor. Trevor said something to Pete. They smiled.

Byron was still panting when we sat on the rock to have our crackers and water.

"How do you do that?" I said.

"Just take off the brakes," he said. "I can't play that song, anyway."

"That's for sure," said Pete. "Where do you take lessons, anyway? Public school?"

Byron put one eyebrow up and one eyebrow down.

"No," he said. "It's not public. You have to live in Puckett Corner."

Pete and Trevor laughed meanly.

"Morgy, today you go to the barn," said Hank Profundo to me. "Go now, because Mr. Shahboz is handing out new music."

"Mr. Shahboz?" I said.

"A conductor from London," said Hank. "He knows the piece and had some time. Very cool you all get to work with him."

"Good luck," said Byron. Clara waved. I went up a path of pine needles and rocks. Pete and Trevor kept laughing. It was hot. My new camp shorts smelled like ironing. My trumpet case banged against my bare legs. Maybe I would like the orchestra. Maybe they needed an extra doof.

In the barn, folding chairs and music stands

were set up around a skinny black-haired man in a black jacket. People were taking instruments out of their cases. They were mostly big kids. Damian sat behind the violinists with his oboe. This orchestra didn't look too junior, except for one kid with a violin who could have been a kindergartner.

Mr. Shahboz made a pencil mark on a piece of music and raised his thin black eyebrows at us. "We begin," he said. "We have this odd concerto, 'Concerto Fabuloso.' Five musicians have solos. Usually, just one solo in a concerto, right? But our composer," and he smiled, as if the composer was being silly, "says they're like his friends in Iran when he was a little boy. Everyone has something to say. Whatever! Five solos. Come up and get your music when I call your name. Mr. MacDougal-MacDuff." I stood up. Damian snorted. "Kindly share your joke," said Mr. Shahboz.

"The joke is Mr. Promising Beginner playing a solo," said Damian.

"A surprise, not a joke. Yes, solos go to experienced players. But here it says 'sounds young, but without mistakes.' We stick to the score. This is our man, I hear." Damian laughed. Mr. Shahboz didn't say anything. He just walked to the back where the trumpets sit and stuck music on my

stand. Then he went up front and called more names. I knew those notes. I tried a couple. When Damian went up to get his music, my music fell off the stand.

"Some solos are more complicated than others, but they go together. You need each other. Like friends," said Mr. Shahboz. I picked up my music and sat down, hard, on the floor. My chair wasn't where it had been. Damian looked at me and tipped up his chin. That was spooky: an orchestra bully.

Mr. Shahboz asked if I was all right. I found my chair and nodded, with tears in my eyes. I wished I had on a hockey helmet with a face guard, also a pillow. "We'll start where we were yesterday. I believe Mr. MacDougal-MacDuff had some coaching this morning." I played along with everyone, just a few notes, and then there was a black bar showing I didn't have to play. I put my trumpet on my knee. For just a moment—three measures—music was everywhere. It was like having headphones on, only better. Then they stopped for the second violins to figure something out. There were a lot of them, so it took a long time. I checked the fire on the other side of the lake. Still burning. A campfire in the daytime? Then Mr. Shahboz said, "Oboe solo?"

Damian stared at the music and the notes flew. He closed his eyes. Bad idea. He gave a little honk-squeak and stopped. "Try again," said Mr. Shahboz, and he hummed a little tune. Damian tried. "Simple isn't easy," said Mr. Shahboz, and made us all play the first part of the little tune together.

Next, the flutist stood up. She had curly black hair. Her flute kept jumping up sideways in her hands as if it were trying to escape. She played OK. She stopped. She stared at the music, did a big trill, then shrugged and sat down. "Enough for today," agreed Mr. Shahboz.

The little violinist stood up. He was taller sitting in his chair. But his fingers spidered up and down the neck of his violin. His bow swooped. He played a long, trembling note. Then he got totally mixed up. A tall girl with a cello almost had it.

"Now you." I heard them turn around to watch, but I just looked at the music. "Not exactly." He hummed the little song. "This solo is the simplest of the simple—not the easiest of the easy. It all builds from here. Go, Mr. Promising Beginner," he said, and he clicked his fingers. The little tune was like feet running up a soccer field, dribbling the ball. It trotted along, and then just when it should have stopped, it didn't. It was like no one caught up with the kid who had the ball. Like Byron said, just take off the brakes. A happy song. I played it.

"Boom, got it, sit down, here we go!" said Mr. Shahboz. Everyone played. The concerto moved along. My ears were hot.

Afterward, one of the other trumpeters, a bigger kid than Damian with a nose diamond, said, "Nice." The third trumpeter gave me a thumbs-up. Waiting for the violinists to get out of the way, I looked over and noticed the fire across the lake was out. Maybe it was a signal. I told Byron about it at lunch, but then Clara came and sat with us and they started playing "Yankee Doodle" with just their mouths, buzzing their lips and humming in a squeaky, trumpet-sounding way.

I wanted to hear my song. In quiet time, I tried just my fingers on the valves. I blew a little air in to see if it sounded right, but Gus said, "Are you signed up for a practice cabin?" I told him no, and that I couldn't remember my solo. He said, "What's the first rule?"

"Play true?" I said.

"No: 'Number one, have fun.' Don't look so worried. Here's a pass; go take a walk. Maybe the barn is empty and you can practice up there." I climbed the hill. In a field next to the barn, a man was wheeling a line marker across the bumpy grass. I watched the white lines for a while to make sure. "Yes!" I said. It was a soccer field.

"Yes!" said the man back to me, and smiled. He had thin black eyebrows and a mustache to match. He kept pushing the line marker. I was all alone on a soccer field. There was even a ball under a bush. I put down my trumpet case and dribbled the ball up to the end. I heard my solo in my head again, the happy little running song. I loved it.

That day, we had soccer for an activity. It was fun. The field wasn't level. The ball kept rolling past the barn. Once it got all the way down to the beach. We had extra kids on the teams who got in the way. But I made a goal. I hadn't played for two years, except when we practiced with Keith's team in California after Savanna and Mike's wedding. I bounced the ball off my knee a couple of times while we walked up to the Outlook for tea.

"Whoa, Morgy got a goal," said Byron. "Do we play the other camp?" he asked Clara.

"What other camp?" she said.

"Those people hiking over there," Byron said.

"I don't know," said Clara. "That's Canada over there."

"Maybe it's a Canadian camp," I said.

"It's a Christmas tree farm," said Damian, sitting down beside Clara, who blushed and said maybe it was Christmas tree farmers hiking. Farmers didn't hike, I thought, and anyway, you wouldn't cut down Christmas trees in summer.

That night, after Gus snapped off the light bulb, I was in bed, looking for the fire. It wasn't there. I was almost asleep. Then I heard a noise. It was someone coming up the dirt road that went behind the cabins. Some tall guy and two shorter guys. I couldn't see who it was through the screens and pine trees. Big kids used the dirt road to get to the wash house. Maybe they got to stay up later than us. These guys were making a clanking noise. The dirt road went all the way up to the main road, next to Bach. Byron was in Bach. What if it was Damian, Pete, and Trevor, doing a prank? I put on my camp sweatshirt over my pajamas and quietly went out after them. It was against the rules, but Byron was probably asleep. I could wake him up before they got to him.

I went straight uphill instead of taking the dirt road. I got to Bach first and sneaked into the cabin.

"Byron," I said. He hit me before he opened his eyes.

"Hey, stop, it's me," I whispered. "I think someone's doing a prank."

"Peanut butter on my pillow?" he said. "They already did. But I put leaves in their beds. Remember when Ferguson used to put leaves down your back?" That was in third grade, but it still made me feel bad thinking about it.

"But I think they're coming back, maybe with a bucket," I said.

Byron got out of bed. We looked out the door.

Then, out on the dirt road, someone said, "Royal Foster, this must be the road. We shall climb up this hill, reconnoiter, and meet up with the regiment."

"'Reconnoiter'? Huh?" said another voice.

"He means 'check it out,' Royal," said a third voice. "And reconnoiter where you're going—you keep stepping on my heel." Byron and I went out on the cabin porch as quickly and quietly as we could. On the dirt road stood the tall guy and two short guys. It wasn't Damian, Pete, and Trevor. They had on three-cornered hats, coats down to their knees, and straps across their chests. The clanking was either their little old-fashioned backpacks, the hatchets in their belts, or the bayonets on their muskets. They disappeared behind a pine tree.

"Whoa," Byron whispered. "Royal who? What did he say about a regiment?" But now someone else was coming up the path. It was Damian, in his bathrobe and Big Bird slippers. He was humming some Beethoven-sounding thing and hitting trees with his toothbrush.

"Doof!" whispered Byron. Damian was heading right for the same pine tree.

"Hey," I whispered. "Damian!" Then the moon came out from behind a cloud.

Damian saw the guys in three-cornered hats and gasped. But they didn't hear him. They were at the main road. They looked both ways, turned right, and ran down it. Byron and I ran up to look. The road was empty and flooded with moonlight.

"Ghosts!" yelled Damian.

"Shh," I said. Ghosts? I thought I could still hear clanking. We stood on the boulder by The Outlook. It was gleaming like noon. The moon went back under clouds. Then, down below, we saw a whole line of soldiers in three-cornered hats marching along where the road comes out from behind some rocks by the lake. *Tap, clink,* they went.

"That must be the regiment," I whispered. "Where are those guys trying to catch up?" Byron shrugged. A little light bobbled out of the woods. Byron grabbed my arm.

"All right," said Byron's counselor, Dan, "what rule did you break?"

"Wait," said Byron, letting go of my arm. "Number two, play true?"

"Have fun?" I said. "Um, we saw some troops reconnoitering, or something."

"Respect! Respect the rules. Number three," said Dan.

Byron said, "Troops, with guns and bayonets."

"What?" said Dan. He shined his flashlight up into the trees overhead.

"He said troops! Troops!" said Damian. "Not squirrels."

"Down there," I pointed after them. But the main road was empty again. "Three of them came up the dirt road," I said. Dan ran down the dirt road, shining his flashlight behind rocks and bushes.

"You'll never find them," said Damian when he came back. "They're ghosts. They vanished."

Dan said *we* weren't ghosts, so what were we doing out of our cabins at ten at night?

"There were some kind of troops or something," I said.

Dan asked if, by any chance, they were wearing three-cornered hats.

"Yes!" said Byron and I.

"OK, Damian," said Dan, "that's enough with the ghost stories. Did Damian tell you about the Lost Band? Revolutionary soldiers that haunt the Outlook? Morgy and Byron, if you need to go to the wash house, get a pass. Otherwise, stay in your cabins, and don't listen to this guy. Damian, what was your scheme? Breaking into the music library and telling a ghost story for an alibi? Or was it the kitchen? I thought even you would want to chill, for your last summer here. Don't scare the younger campers."

"I wasn't scared!" said Byron.

"It was ghosts," said Damian. "I was practicing my solo and I forgot to brush my teeth and I saw them. I've been coming here for eight years and I finally saw them!"

"For being out at ten without a pass, you all get lunch duty tomorrow," said Dan.

"We're being haunted and you talk about lunch," said Damian.

Dan said if ghosts were real, we would really have to respect the rules, and him. He gave Damian one more chance to admit he made the whole thing up. Then he said he would have to call another counselor and search the camp, since the colonel was in Boston. Meanwhile, we should go back to our cabins and hope they did find troops, ghosts, or even a convincing raccoon, because we had lunch duty if they didn't.

"Troops!" he said, walking Damian back to Beethoven.

"I wonder if they ever reconnoitered," Byron said when he climbed into Bach. In Mozart, Gus and everyone were still asleep. I lay down in my bed. Dan and another counselor went by with flashlights. I couldn't see the light over in Canada tonight. Just Dad's clock.

FOUR

Royal's Friend's Spur

Morgo!
Here are the funny papers. Are you OK up there? Your uncle Mike is right nearby at smokejumper camp. I miss you both! See you on the Fourth of July.
Savanna

I wondered for just a minute what my aunt Savanna had planned for the Fourth of July, and where the smokejumper camp was. But then the kitchen door swung open and Donna, the cook, was crooking her finger at us to come in and do our work. It was right after lunch. She had a white apron, green rubber clogs, bright pink rubber gloves, and a hairnet over curly gray hair. "Damian," she said, "you sure don't waste any time getting people in trouble."

We had to wear hairnets, aprons, and rubber gloves, too. But it was just us and Donna, so no one made fun of us. Well, I laughed at Byron because his hair was sticking up through his hairnet. He squirted some dish detergent at me, but Mrs. Profundo, with an apron but no hairnet, came in and asked if we wanted to buy a whole new bottle of dish detergent. We said no, and stopped.

"Just do your job," said Donna. "We have a cookout on the Fourth of July, and you do not want to scrub the grills or fill ketchup bottles."

She sent us outside to pick up apple cores and glasses while she washed the knives left over from making sandwiches. Some of the glasses still had milk in them. Some had apple cores, napkins, wet sandwich crusts, and milk. The glop went in the garbage can. We put the dry cores and crusts into a bucket for Mrs. Profundo's chickens. We put the glasses into trays that went into a huge dishwasher named Hobie, which was almost as tall as a refrigerator. We did the same with plates, about a

MT. LEBANON PUBLIC LIBRARY

million. Donna showed me how to sweep the floor cracks sideways to get the crumbs out. Damian wiped the counters. Byron put lids on peanut butter tubs and put big cans of jam and pickles back in the refrigerator. I washed cookie sheets.

Donna went to the pantry. Damian hung up his apron and hairnet and ran out the door. Byron closed the fridge. I hung up the broom. Donna backed into the room dragging a big bag of flour. Byron and I picked up the other end of the bag and helped drag it over to the counter. She punched a little door in the countertop and it flipped open. She poured the flour through the door into a bin underneath.

"Huh. Left already, did he?" said Donna. "You guys shouldn't listen to Damian. He gets everyone in trouble," she said. "And it looks like this'll be our last summer."

"But it was us," I said. "We saw the troops."

"Troops!" She laughed. We told her we did see troops, old-fashioned ones, with guns, bayonets, and hatchets. "Get out of here," she said. "Old-fashioned troops? The Lost Band? You've been around that campfire too long, listening to ghost stories."

We said they weren't ghosts, they were real. She

said, "Whatever," but then she told us a story about the Lost Band. They were a small band of soldiers that spent the night around here in the Revolutionary War. They were hiding out from some Canadian and British troops. A regiment that came to help them never found them. They were called the Lost Band, and they were supposed to still haunt the Outlook. Other campers sometimes thought they saw troops, too. "But let's face it," she said. "A lot of these little prodigies are away from Mommy and Daddy for the first time. They're going to have all kinds of nightmares."

"Huh," said Byron. "We've been to California, and I go to hockey camp."

Donna said not to get her wrong; she could tell we weren't prodigies. "I'm just saying I hear this story a lot, usually after chili night." She thought kids who ate too much chili got indigestion and had nightmares. The bugle blew for practice and quiet time. "But could you do me a favor and take the bucket to the chicken coop? It's just down the road—cut across the graveyard. Mrs. Profundo forgot to come back for it."

We went down the road, through a gate in a stone wall, and across the graveyard. "Chili night," Byron said. "I didn't even know that stuff was chili.

Gross! I just had crackers." The graveyard was sunny, with birds singing and brown, crispy pine needles underfoot. The gravestones had curved tops and lichen growing on them. Lichen tells you the air isn't polluted, Byron said. Some of the gravestones were tipped over. Some had little American flags with thirteen stars in a circle, because the people buried there were in the Revolutionary War. I saw another glass from lunch, sitting on a rock under a pine tree. I went to get it. The grave next to it said, ROYAL FOSTER, GENERAL BLODGETT'S REGIMENT and it had two flags stuck in.

"Whoa," said Byron. "Remember, someone said that name, Royal Foster. And the regiment, they had to join up with the regiment."

"Well," I said, "I don't believe in ghosts."

"It wasn't the chili, because I didn't have any," said Byron. "Maybe it was time travelers!" We stepped over the other stone wall and there was the chicken coop.

"Thank you, boys," said Mrs. Profundo. "I'm sorry to have spoken sharply to you about the dish detergent, but we have to watch our pennies. Are you the promising beginners?"

"Yes," I said.

"I just talked to the colonel on the phone. He's in Boston. He was sorry to hear you had lunch duty."

"Sorry," I said, "we were out of our cabins at night. We thought we saw someone on the dirt road behind the cabins."

"Goodness," she said. "They're supposed to call me."

"Ghosts call you?" said Byron.

"No, dear, campers from Camp Happy Pines in Skiffwood. They have big 'capture the flag' games all night sometimes, and they use the road to get to the lake. It used to be the way everyone got down to the lake. But they're supposed to let me know, because it goes so close to the cabins."

"Whoa, cool," said Byron. "Capture the flag!"

Mrs. Profundo said, in a sort of mad way, that Happy Pines was very different from Outlook. She would tell the colonel, because we shouldn't get in trouble for that. "He doesn't like the scholarship students having to work. He had to be a waiter up here when he was a boy. He says to behave yourselves and pay your way with your music. Oh, and doesn't one of you run awfully well? He said you should be in the Fourth of July road race; see if we can win for once instead of Happy Pines." She took the pail of scraps into the chicken coop.

"That's you," I said to Byron on the way back down the hill. By the road, just across from the Outlook, something glinted in the weeds. Byron went over and picked it up.

"Look," he said. It was a piece of metal in a U shape, with a little spike and a leather strap. "I think it's from one of their boots. A spur, or something."

"I bet it's Royal's," I said.

"Royal's friend's," said Byron. "Remember, Royal kept stepping on his heel?" He put it in his pocket. "'Capture the flag'? I don't think so."

I didn't either.

FIVE
Parades

Dear Morgy,

Miss Merriweather had a yard sale and we bought a big fan. Dante and Pancake lie in front of it all day. Do you remember the Fourth of July parade last year? You and Savanna took the babies and the fire engine made so much noise you all cried. Is it hot up there, too? Go swimming!

Love,

Mom

P.S. Savanna will be up to see you on the Fourth!

It wasn't hot; it was raining. We swam to the island anyway, because it was a special day-before-the-Fourth-of-July camp tradition. As long as there was no thunder, it was fine, said the colonel, and jumped in. Even Mrs. Profundo and Donna swam.

Snack was inside the Outlook, and we got cocoa. There was sand on the floor from the beach, and the little kids' teeth were chattering. After we got dressed, the marching band practiced on the beach. Byron was better. He still looked at the kid next to him all the time to make sure he had the right note, though. Huh, I thought. That kid could have been me.

Clara was in the front row with some other flutes and piccolos. She didn't look at anyone but the leader, her flute didn't fly up, and she stayed in step. She had on the serious look that kept people from laughing at her when she read lunch menus at school, and a black three-cornered hat. *Thump, thump, thump, thump,* went their feet on the wet sand in march time. I wished I were better at marching.

In junior orchestra we worked on "Concerto Fabuloso" with Ms. Rapontin. Mr. Shahboz had to fly back to London to conduct something. The violins had some trouble. We kept getting off the beat that sounded like someone running, which Ms. Rapontin called a pulse. I played a wrong note and we had to start over. My solo had to be right, Ms. Rapontin said, because it was the first one. Plus, Damian said, a trumpet is as loud as sixteen violins and sounds way worse when it's off-key. Ms. Rapontin told him to mind his own business and me to practice, but not let it get old. Damian shook his head. His solo, with way more notes, was perfect. It was just like hockey. I was the one who made everyone sigh.

At lunch, we sat on the warm boulder. Byron played "Yankee Doodle" with just his mouth. Clara kicked her heels against the boulder in march time. They were excited. They got to wear blue jackets and white knee pants and march in three different parades for little towns close by that didn't have high school bands. Some didn't even have high schools. Some places were so small that Outlook's marching band would be the whole parade.

Today they were in a parade in Elm Quarters, on the other side of the lake. They were going on a bus. On the way back, they would stop and play in the Beaver City bandstand and then march up a road to a hotel where people loved to hear band music. Tomorrow, the Fourth, they had a parade in Skiffwood. That was where they held the road race.

During quiet time, the practice rooms were full. I stood under a big tree in the woods above the barn and played my song. Now I could see a rectangle of people on the beach across the lake. It was far away, but the sand was light. I thought I could see black hats. Three-cornered ones. There were a lot of them, and a double line of white tents. I didn't think it could be campers or Christmas tree farmers. It had to be the troops we saw marching down the lake road that night. Maybe they were getting ready for a parade, too. I wondered if anyone here would notice. They were all so busy practicing for their own parades. The Fourth of July was like Christmas if you were in a marching band. And just boring and lonely if you were in junior orchestra.

At home when I'm lonely, Dante cheers me up. When it's time for a walk, he runs down the stairs and skids on the hall rug. And Pancake takes a cat bath on my homework or bats my toy cars around. Up here, all I had was those troops.

I pretended I could play loud enough for Dante to hear. He loves the trumpet. *Broot! Ta-da breet*

breet, toot! I began. All I did wrong in rehearsal was to forget the G-sharp. Pretty wrong, but easy to fix. *Broooooooot, ta da!* Pancake runs out of the room with his ears down no matter what I play. I missed those guys.

At soccer I told Byron about the troops. From the field we could see them marching off the beach. "Is that a parade, or should we tell someone?" I said. We always played defense. We liked passing to each other. Clouds were blowing away. The sky was blue. "They're not going to attack or anything, are they?" I said.

"Only if they're time travelers," said Byron, and then we had to run way back. The big trumpet player, our goalie, dived and pushed the ball away from our goal. Byron ran over to it and nudged it, getting ready to kick it. But someone from the other team got it away from him. The ball hit a grass clump and popped up to me. My old coach in second grade would go, "Boot it, Morgy!" The good old days. California, Keith on my team, a flat field, no troops, no mosquitoes. I booted it right over the other team, to our forwards.

We rushed up to the middle line, then to the goal. I heard my solo, the happy little running song, in my head. Pete, a forward, tried to get the ball in. It hit the side of the goal and shot up in the air. It came flying down like a meteorite. I stood under it and waited. I closed my eyes, kept my chin down, and then—bonk!—I hit it with my head. Byron got it and kicked it in.

"Yes!" said everyone. "Yes!" said Pete, but he didn't high-five Byron. He remembered those leaves in his bed. Running back to my position, I was playing my solo with my mouth. *"Broot ta-da breet breet, toot!"* It went with soccer. The man with the mustache who put the lines on the field heard me. He gave me a thumbs-up.

At tea, we told Clara about the troops. She said, "It's a parade." Then we told her about the soldiers on the dirt road that night, and reconnoitering. "We should tell the colonel," she said.

I said, "Maybe Mrs. Profundo is up by the chicken coop. We took the scraps up there to her when we had lunch duty. She could call him in Boston."

Byron said, "Let's go now." Clara slid off the boulder and walked up the road. We followed.

"Morgy saw them on the beach on the other side of the lake when he was up in the woods practicing," said Byron. "Now they're marching around the lake."

"So these are the same ones you saw when you

got in trouble for being out of your cabins at night?" Clara said. I showed her Royal Foster's grave. Byron still had the spur. We went uphill, where we could see. Byron and I definitely saw bayonets and three-cornered hats. Clara wasn't sure. We climbed over the other stone wall. The chickens were pecking in their coop.

"Look," said Clara, "we don't need to ask Mrs. Profundo to call the colonel." Behind some rosebushes was a little house with a lawn. The colonel and Mrs. Profundo were sitting on lawn chairs, holding hands. "We should leave them alone," Clara whispered.

"Popsy, we have no choice," the colonel was saying. "It's Mrs. Saybrook's property. She is the chairman of the board. She could make a million and a half dollars on the vacation condos. We only made a hundred and fifty dollars this summer. They're all coming up for an emergency meeting. The developer's coming, too. It doesn't look good."

"Only a hundred and fifty dollars? How can it be so little?" said Mrs. Profundo.

"It doesn't start out little, does it? All the parents pay us for camp, plus the special funding from that anonymous donor for the promising beginners. They even got their sweatshirt money in on time.

That's a lot. But then, we pay Donna and the counselors and teachers, buy food and supplies, and remember we had to get the truck fixed? And it's never cheap getting music copied and having the pianos tuned, and insurance. It all adds up. Actually, it's all subtraction! Tuition, funding, and sweatshirt money minus all our expenses equals one hundred and fifty dollars."

"But sell the Outlook? I just can't imagine that," said Mrs. Profundo. "We did make that money selling eggs."

"Yes, forty-nine dollars," he said. "Without your chickens, the profit would only have been one hundred and one dollars. Maybe less, because of the eggs we ate free! And this year we have our best marching band ever. Clean and crisp, no nonsense. They love to march, they love to practice. Wait till they see the people in Elm Quarters all lined up on Main Street, just to hear them. They'll never want to stop. If you add that in, we made a huge profit this year!" I was getting embarrassed, and I wasn't even in the marching band.

"Shh," said Mrs. Profundo. "Here come the promising beginners and Clara."

"Excuse me," said Clara. "This is Byron and Morgy, and they think we might be under attack."

"Ha!" said the colonel. "We are! Real estate going up, price of gas, price of food, musical kids have to eat, we need a new porch, not to mention Mrs. Saybrook, God bless her, and the special board meeting this week. We certainly are under attack."

"No," I said, "soldiers, with three-cornered hats, and guns. They're all over the other side of the lake, they have tents, and they're marching this way. One night some of them went right by our cabins on the dirt road. They have bayonets."

"Oh, for goodness' sakes," said Mrs. Profundo. She went in the house and got some binoculars. "Hiram, it's reenactors."

The colonel said some people like history so much, they dress up like soldiers and act out battles on weekends. Sometimes they even set up an encampment, just like in history. "It's that lost band of soldiers," he said. "Drives the historians crazy. During the Revolutionary War, a small band of American soldiers attacked Canada. But Canada, and some redcoats, fought back. So the Americans had to hide out in the Outlook till the Canadians went away. Another regiment—General Blodgett's—came to help. Blodgett and his men never did find them. So they're called the Lost Band. Silly to attack Canada in the first place. We'd just been defeated trying to take over Quebec. But there's a folk song about that little band of soldiers. The story goes that the Outlook is haunted." He looked across the lake again. "There are too many of them to be the Lost Band. They must be reenacting General Blodgett's Regiment."

"They are," I said. "That's what it says on Royal Foster's gravestone. Plus, the soldiers said they were reconnoitering to catch up with the regiment."

"Are they attacking?" said Clara.

"They shouldn't," said the colonel. "The Outlook is an old American stronghold."

Crack! Crack! Crack! There was gray smoke down there, from the guns.

"Hmm," said the colonel. "Anyway, they don't use bullets. But we should tell the campers. Morgy, get on the boulder by the dining room and play reveille. The band should leave early for the parades with all this foot traffic. Byron, climb up on top of the Outlook and put this on the flagpole—we surrender!" He gave Byron Mrs. Profundo's white hanky.

I didn't know how to play reveille, so I played "Pop! Goes the Weasel," loud. Everyone came over to the boulder. Damian was laughing. Down the hill

came the colonel. Mrs. Profundo and Clara followed him. Clara had on her three-cornered hat. She just looked at Damian and he shut up. The colonel told the marching band to get their instruments, suit up, and get on the bus.

"Pay no attention to gunshots. Ho-ho! I haven't heard that command for a while," he said. "But don't worry. There's an army marching on us. They're pretending it's still the Revolutionary War. It's not," he said to the little blond girl who lit the campfire the first night. He patted her head. *Crack!* Another shot. She opened a case. She took out a piccolo. Clara handed her a hat and coat. Kids got blue coats and three-cornered hats from Clara and white knee pants from Mrs. Profundo. They got on the bus.

Donna came running out of the kitchen. "Mrs. Profundo, Mrs. Saybrook's train just arrived," she said. "She's waiting at the station in Beaver City."

"Oh, deary me," said Mrs. Profundo. "Can you or Hank drive down and get her?"

Byron yelled down that the troops were on our side of the lake now.

Hank Profundo said, "They're marching four across up that little lake road. Can you phone Mrs. Saybrook and ask her to wait?"

But Donna said Mrs. Saybrook called from the pay phone at the station.

"We play at Elm Quarters in forty-five minutes. How can the band bus get through if a car can't?" said the band leader, whose ponytail looked old-fashioned sticking out from under his three-cornered hat, even though one side of his knee pants wasn't covering his bright blue bicycle shorts.

"Walk, if you have to," said the colonel. "We have a parade. Could be one of our last." The band leader started the bus engine. Ms. Rapontin came down from her office with a three-cornered hat on.

"Another grownup, good," said Mrs. Profundo as Ms. Rapontin got on. "You go, too, Hank, dear."

Byron climbed down off the roof, grabbed his trumpet case and outfit, and got on the bus. Hank got on and sat next to Ms. Rapontin. *Crack!* It was the bus doors closing.

Practically the whole junior orchestra was watching from the boulder, with the colonel. The reenactors were now marching up our side of the lake. They had their three-cornered hats. Their bayonet blades shone in the sun. The bus disappeared down the hill. Then it showed up again, just beyond the rocks. Along came the troops. The bus stopped.

We could see the bus door open. The band leader, Ms. Rapontin, and Hank Profundo got out. A soldier on a horse rode up to the front of the troops. They talked to him. He pointed his sword uphill. The soldiers didn't move. Hank and Ms. Rapontin got back in the bus. The band leader stayed, but the soldier on horseback didn't move. The band leader started back to the bus. The colonel put his binoculars down. Everyone was quiet, thinking about the last parades, and the Outlook sign being taken down, and how we should keep playing. Colonel Profundo sighed. Help, I thought.

Then down by the bus a black van drove out of a trail the woods. The horse skittered. A woman got out of the van. The soldier pointed his sword again. She didn't move. She patted the horse's nose. The soldier turned to the troops. They took a step to the side and put the stocks of their muskets down by their feet. "At ease, men," said the colonel, who was looking through the binoculars again. "What now?"

The soldier got off his horse and unfolded a piece of paper. Another woman got out of the van. They all looked at the paper. A man in jeans ran up from behind the soldiers and unrolled another paper. The first woman got something out of the van.

"They're checking their maps," said the colonel. The soldier got back on the horse. Then, several things happened at once. The women got back into the van. A soldier ran and got in, too. The van turned around and backed into the woods on the other side of the road. The bus pulled over. The band got out. The troops stepped aside. The band marched through the middle of them and went down the road. The soldier on horseback held up his sword and the troops began to march again.

"Well, they can get to Elm Quarters on foot," said the colonel, looking at his watch. "But what's become of our bus, and who were those ladies?" There was a sound of tree branches scraping and snapping. The van backed out of the beach path, turned around, drove up the field, and parked in the parking lot. The van looked familiar, even with pine branches stuck in the windshield wipers. The soldier got out.

The colonel saluted. So did the soldier. But the colonel wasn't saluting him. He was saluting a woman who stepped out the side door. The soldier politely gave her his hand. She was dressed in blue from the little hat on top of her gray hair down to her matching pointy high heels.

"Mrs. Saybrook," said the colonel. "So nice of you to come early."

The driver set the emergency brake and climbed out. She was wearing a T-shirt with a lobster in a firefighter's hat on it, and cutoffs. "Sorry," she said. "I think I took out a couple of your branches. The van goes better in reverse on these steep hills." Then she noticed me and said, "Morgo!" She gave me the big, hard hug my aunt Savanna always gives me, no matter where we are, or who is watching, until the smell of her perfume—like jungle flowers and hot sauce—makes me sneeze.

"Ah-choo!"

"Colonel," said Mrs. Saybrook, "I don't know what I would have done without Mrs. Noonan here. She was in Beaver City when I arrived and offered me a ride." My aunt, who got called "Banana McDoof" in third grade, was now Mrs. Noonan.

"We had to take fire trails!" said Savanna.

"'General Blodgett' sends apologies," said the soldier. "We didn't know you were here. We scouted up a dirt road a couple of weeks ago. We went right by the cabins, but it was so quiet, and we heard the property was being sold. We thought the camp was closed." He had only one spur. "We're extras on a television show called *History Mysteries,* which solves historical riddles. They're researching the Lost Band."

"That musketry was not the work of extras," said the colonel.

The soldier thanked him and said yes, they were reenactors of General Blodgett's Regiment. They were following an old map they'd found in his papers. "We always wanted to retrace the regiment's path when they tried to rescue the Lost Band, and this show gave us a chance," he said. "Before the condos are built."

"Well, if that's their path, General Blodgett's Regiment was lost, not the Lost Band!" said Mrs. Saybrook.

"Old, old map," said Savanna.

The soldier said they knew it was a bad map. It might have been made by the British to confuse the Americans. But that was the map the regiment actually used. They were reenactors and they couldn't change history. "But when we saw Mrs. Noonan's fire service map, we could tell we were lost in real life, too," he said. "We thought we were camped at the other end of the lake, but we were actually in Canada, behind enemy lines."

Mrs. Saybrook said well, the lake looks the same upside down as right side up, and even the modern satellite map they had was confusing. The soldier said, right side up or not, they should have waited till camp was closed. He was very sorry about the shooting.

"Did you solve your History Mystery?" said Savanna.

He said they learned a lot. For example, they set signal fires to show the Lost Band that help was on the way. But, going by the map, they lit them in Canada. The Lost Band would have thought more Canadian and British troops were coming to get them. They still didn't know exactly what happened to the Lost Band, but they probably weren't lost—in battle or in geography. "They lived around here, so they knew their way around. Maybe they escaped."

I said, "I saw the signal fires from my cabin. Also, my friend has your spur."

"Where is your friend?" he said.

"Walking to Elm Quarters," I said.

Mrs. Saybrook said, "The road was closed so they could tape the TV show. The general said the band had to wait till the soldiers were finished. Well! They would have been late. But Mrs. Noonan had a word with him, and finally the children marched to their parade. Very stirring. They were playing 'Yankee Doodle'—could you hear them? That should save something on gas. I invited the soldiers to come hear our orchestra in the barn. I hope that will be all right."

The colonel, who had been smiling through the whole story, stopped smiling. We had no conductor. Ms. Rapontin was with the band. But Mrs. Profundo said, "Yes, Mrs. Saybrook, that will be fine. We'll set out chairs in front of the barn for the regiment, and Mr. Shahboz can conduct."

"Mr. Shahboz?" said the colonel. We all knew Mr. Shahboz was in London. But Donna and Mrs. Profundo were already on their way up to the barn to set out chairs. So we got our instruments.

Maybe it would be our last concert, too.

SIX
Concerto Fabuloso

We put all the dining room chairs on the hillside for the reenactors. The man with the mustache who made the lines for soccer came and pushed the barn doors all the way open. We turned our orchestra chairs to face out the door. The barn was our stage. He brought us our stands and we put our music on them.

Tap, clink, tap, clink, tap, clink, reenactors were marching up the road. The short violinist played an A. We tuned up. Here they came up to the barn. Up close, they didn't look like an army. They had all different colored knee pants and shirts and coats. Their black hats were kind of floppy, with the sides pinned up. But they all had hatchets and guns with bayonets, and they all looked serious.

They had straps over their chests with pouches for bullets, I guess, or gunpowder. They had old-looking backpacks with rolled-up blankets. They leaned their guns against each other in threes and sat down. Some guys with jeans on put TV cameras on a rock. The colonel stood in front of us.

"It is a pleasure to welcome General Blodgett's Regiment back to the Outlook after all these years," he said. "For Independence Day it's customary to play patriotic music from our country's illustrious past. Today we will hear 'Concerto Fabuloso,' by a newcomer to our country, played by musicians you'll be hearing from in the future. Mr. Shahboz, if you please."

Maybe Mr. Shahboz was back. We looked around. Then, "I can't believe it," whispered Damian to the clarinetist, "we've got that janitor for a conductor."

The man with the mustache, the one who opened the barn doors and brought us our music stands, and who also marked the soccer field, now took the baton, tapped it, made sure we were paying attention, and signaled us to begin the concerto.

The violins played the beginning part, and got it right. We joined the violins where the music gave a hint of the little running song. A couple of soldiers were leaning back in their chairs for a nap, with their black hats tipped forward over their eyes. I was concentrating on my notes, but I was also laughing to myself. The next part was all kettledrums, like bombs falling. It was so scary and noisy, the reenactors were going to think the redcoats were coming. I couldn't watch them, though. I had to look at the music and watch for my solo.

It really was the easiest one in the concerto, even if simple wasn't easy. Plus, I was way in the back. And the little running song was even more of a surprise than the drums. No one who wasn't in the orchestra could know it was coming. But the man with the mustache knew. He was smiling at me the measure before I stood up.

Mr. Shahboz called it "the silver lining." Probably because, right when I played, the drummer started hitting silver tubes instead of drums. It was all the happy running song from then on. It sounded even happier than we rehearsed—and faster. When I sat down, I was invisible again. That was my silver lining.

The man with the mustache had each kid who had a solo stand at just the right time. Each one was harder till Damian's, the hardest. The violinist made a mistake, and the flutist was too quiet when

she started off, but we stayed on our running-feet beat. It seemed to go fast and slow at the same time. Like a big long run down a soccer field you can't believe you get to do. No one can stop you. And it's like slow motion. You're running and running, but it's over way too fast. And suddenly Damian finished, perfectly. It was quiet. The man with the mustache looked almost sad. Then he turned around.

First it was only the colonel, Mrs. Profundo, and Savanna clapping. Then General Blodgett's Regiment started to clap. Then they stomped on the ground and Mrs. Saybrook and Savanna stood up. Then they all stood up, still clapping.

The man with the mustache motioned for me to come up to the front of the orchestra to take a bow. Then came the violinist, the cellist, the flutist, and finally Damian, who flourished his hand as he bowed. They loved Damian. The conductor held up his hand and showed him off to the audience. Then all the soloists bowed. The conductor mopped his face with a handkerchief as the whole orchestra stood. One more bow. Then the colonel said, "Our composer, Mr. Shahboz." He bowed all by himself. More applause.

"Encore!" someone yelled, so Damian played his solo again. Then they all got up and stood around. Donna and Mrs. Profundo passed trays of graham crackers. Our conductor started for the back door of the barn.

"Wait," said Damian, "you're not Mr. Shahboz. He's the famous conductor."

"He is. I am Cyrus Shahboz, the composer, and my brother, Darius Shahboz, the conductor, is getting famous," said the man. "You're quite right about that."

"Don't they pay composers very much? Is that why you had to mark the soccer field and rake the beach and get chairs and stuff?" said the little violinist.

He laughed. "You played so well. Sorry not to rehearse you, and now to leave. I am just shy. My brother is not, so he kindly helped out. The colonel didn't want me working on the fields. But I was here anyway, not conducting, so I helped out." He shrugged. "You all understand my concerto, I see. It is about friends." Damian was signing an autograph for one of the soldiers.

"It's about soccer," I said.

"And bombs going off, right?" said the drummer. "And you kept playing."

"And you were OK," said the violinist.

"Actually, you were very happy, because you all got through it together," said the flutist.

"Who told you?" said Mr. Cyrus Shahboz, and touched her cheek. He tried to get out the door, but a cameraman, Mrs. Saybrook, and the reenactor with the missing spur surrounded him and shook his hand. Savanna gave me a hug. "You and your solos!" she said. Everyone looked at me like, He plays solos? But she was just talking about when we played at her wedding and Byron and Keith didn't know the rest of the song.

Mrs. Profundo brought us our own tray of graham crackers and we sat on the boulder together. "Are the smokejumpers having a parade, too?" I asked.

"They'll march in the Skiffwood parade. I was down at Beaver City picking up their banner and a big box of freeze pops for them to hand out."

"You came all the way up here to pick up a banner and some freeze pops?" I said. She said she wasn't about to miss a parade that had me, Byron, and Uncle Mike in it. "Plus, I missed Mike." Reenactors were everywhere. One was taking a nap by one of Mrs. Profundo's rosebushes. One was sitting on the porch swing talking to the colonel. Some others were throwing a Frisbee with a picture of Bach on it. It landed by us. The general, whose horse was tethered to the Outlook porch, came to get it, and bowed to Savanna. "All's well that ends well," he said as he picked it up. Savanna smiled.

"What did you say to him back there?" I said.

"Well, I was just patting his horse," said Savanna. "I told him the horse looked like some polo ponies I know. And he said he knew people who played polo. So I said, even in a rough game like that, you have to be a good sport. He said, of course, why didn't the kids go first? I said they could probably walk if the bus bothered him, as long as it wasn't too far to Elm Quarters. Then they all got out their maps to see how far it was. We looked on my fire Service map, and there they were, on the wrong end of the lake. Pf," she added, which is a noise she makes when people are being ridiculous. The Frisbee landed at her feet again and she jumped up and threw it to the general.

"Hey!" said Travis, the violin soloist. "That's my Bach Frisbee."

"Sorry," said a reenactor. "I just found it." The general threw it to Travis. The band bus drove up.

"Whoa," said Byron, running up and catching

the Frisbee before I could. "They did have bayonets. They made us walk because they didn't have buses then. At least we could get back in and ride up that hill at the end." Bach's head whizzed away.

"Huh," I said. "We had to play 'Concerto Fabuloso' for them."

"Hey, promising beginners, smile," said Damian. The cameramen were filming us, even though, Byron pointed out, they didn't have Frisbees then, either, especially dorky ones with Bach on them. Royal Foster's friend laughed. Byron gave him back his spur. Mrs. Profundo announced that the regiment was invited for supper. "We have plenty to go around," she said. "It's chili night."

Donna winked at me and Byron.

Dear Mom,
Tell the girls not to be afraid of the fire sirens. It's only a parade.
Morgy

SEVEN
This Last Week

Dear Morgy,
We think we can see the fireworks from your room! Phoebe is trying to say your name. Dante misses you. See you soon!

Love,
Mom

The *o*'s in the word *soon* had smiley faces.

At camp, we could see the fireworks that Happy Pines sent up. Pete said it was a much bigger camp that had international soccer stars for coaches, but not any music. The Fourth of July parade was in Skiffwood. The reenactors marched behind the band in their dress uniforms: blue coats, white pants, and stiff three-cornered hats. The cameramen filmed from a car. Then came the junior orchestra. We played in the back of the camp truck. We could only fit if our drummer left the kettledrums and silver tubes in the barn and marched with the marching band. We played the Outlook song. Ms. Rapontin said "Concerto Fabuloso" ought to be played sitting still, and anyway, people who watched the parade were used to the Outlook song.

The little kids on the sidewalks liked it best when we played "Pop! Goes the Weasel" and Ms. Rapontin, in the passenger seat, threw Tootsie Rolls out the window. The smokejumpers marched behind us, carrying their Pulaski trenching tools, which are shovels for digging fire breaks. Uncle Mike waved at me. Savanna handed out freeze pops at the end. Byron won the Skiffwood road race. The reenactors went back to their camp, and we had our cookout.

Donna was right: the cookout was a lot of work. There was a big grill and you could sit anywhere, so aferward it took forever to find all the glasses and ketchup bottles and corncobs. We didn't have to help clean up, but Ms. Rapontin told Byron that it would be nice, since a lot of the counselors were at a battle of bands in Vermont and the colonel and Mrs. Profundo were down in Beaver City, picking up more board members for the meeting.

Donna scraped the grill. "You kids go on down to campfire," she said. "Hank can take these corncobs up to the chicken coop tomorrow in the truck." That was good news. They were all in a garbage can that looked very heavy. Donna slowly walked up to the kitchen with a dishtowel over her shoulder. She looked sad. So did Hank, standing by the pile of wood that was going to be the campfire.

"They won't shut us down. I was too good," said Damian. Byron crooked his eyebrow like, Only one more week. The little girl with blond hair came down the path last. Hank Profundo gave her a piccolo, and she played a sparkly little song. Clara said it was from *The Nutcracker Suite,* like the song Damian played the first night.

No one even breathed till it was over. "That's how it's supposed to sound," said Clara sadly. "He forgot. He's supposed to give you an instrument you don't usually play." Everyone was very quiet, even the big guys who played trumpet with me in orchestra.

Byron, who had gotten to campfire first, even though no one else raced, lit the fire. Sparks flew up into the dark sky. Across the lake, there was a signal fire from General Blodgett's Regiment. We sang "Bye Bye, Blackbird," the song about the cowboy who loved you so true, and another sad one about the wide Missouri.

Then we sang "I've Been Working on the Railroad," but we changed it from "Dinah, won't you blow your horn" to "Donna, won't you blow your horn," and those same big guys from orchestra and I stood up and blew our trumpets every time. That was better—not so sad. And we finished with the Outlook song. "Outlook, Ou-out-look, look out, each day starts with a SHOUT!" we all yelled at the end. Then we lined up to go back to our cabins.

"Whoa!" said Gus when we got up to the Outlook.

"Robbers?" said Byron. It looked like a crime scene. The lid was off the garbage can. It was upside down. Corncobs were all over the ground, and the grill lay on its side. The porch swing was dangling upside down in its chains. The porch door was open, but the kitchen lights were out.

"Donna?" yelled Damian. "Donna, are you in there? We have to rescue her. Her room is right behind that swing." Then we heard someone shuffling around. Some glass broke. The window behind the porch swing opened quietly. Donna climbed out, looked over her shoulder, and ran down the porch stairs faster than even Byron.

"It's a bear," she told Hank. "We should never have left those corncobs out. There were two bears. I hit the garbage can and scared one away, but this one got confused and ran into the dining room. This is all we need right now." Her voice wobbled.

"We've had bears before," said Hank, patting her fuzzy back. She had on a pink *101 Dalmatians* bathrobe.

"But not inside, and not with Mrs. Saybrook in the top bedroom!"

Way up in the tower where we had lessons with Ms. Rapontin, one light was on. Downstairs in the dining room, chairs were moving and falling over.

"This can't be happening to us! Call the police!" said Damian. Gus told him to calm down. Then I thought of something. Our trumpets. I explained to Hank about Dante and Pancake. Either the bear would like the trumpet, like Dante, or he would hate it, like Pancake.

Damian yelled that it was a bear, not a house pet, and he didn't even believe that about Dante.

Byron told him to shut up about Dante, but Hank didn't seem to be listening to them. He said it didn't matter if the bear liked the trumpet or hated it. Either way, it would probably be good. But if bears liked the trumpet, we should probably be able to get out of the way. We would play in the camp truck with the motor running, so he could drive away if the bear ran after us. Just to be on the safe side, he said, even though American black bears are pretty shy. "Shy!" yelled Damian.

Hank ran and got the truck. Byron and I and the big guys from orchestra all got in back with our trumpets. Then Gerry Ann got in with her trombone, and another girl from band handed up her tuba and climbed in. Gus made everyone else go down to the parking lot.

CRASH! came from inside. Then the sound of glass breaking.

"Oh, dear," said Donna. "That must be the milk glasses."

"What shall we play?" said Byron. "'God Rest Ye'?"

"Shut up and play, promising beginners!" yelled Damian from the parking lot.

We played "God Rest Ye Merry, Gentlemen," "Pop! Goes the Weasel," and "Twinkle, Twinkle."

At least, I think that's what we played. We didn't talk. We just tried to all play the same thing. It was quiet after "Twinkle." Then there was another crash and a tearing noise. The bear came out through the screen, walked along the porch on all fours, looked at us over its shoulder, jumped off, and jogged into the woods.

Donna jumped up on the porch and turned the lights on. We went in and started picking up chairs. Hank found a broom. Donna came out of the kitchen and said she was so glad she left the cocoa mugs in the dishwasher. Everything else was broken. We would be seeing a lot of those mugs. Meanwhile, we should have some cocoa and go to bed. We sat on the part of the dining room floor that Hank had swept. The kettle whistled.

"Remember at school, we were sitting on the floor in the cafeteria when we first heard her play?" said Byron, watching Ms. Rapontin bring in a tray.

"Nice job out there, boys," she said, handing us our mugs. "I can see you've made the most of camp. But Byron, I should oil your valves again. Tomorrow we'll have our lesson in the barn, because Mrs. Saybrook is staying in our classroom. It was her room when she was a little girl."

"You mean she went to camp here?" I said.

"No," said Ms. Rapontin. "Outlook was her grandfather's farm. Her uncle started the camp, but the rest of the family always came for summer vacation."

"Great cocoa," said Byron. He was the only person smiling. He couldn't help it. He loved it when Ms. Rapontin paid attention to him. We all lined up with our cabins to go to bed. Ms. Rapontin told Hank she would help him with the dining room. Hank said, "I guess if we work all night, we'll get it cleaned up enough for this last week." He thought the bear was probably trying to eat the carpenter ants in the porch. "The condo guys will thank her. She got the demolition started for them."

"He doesn't mean that," said Ms. Rapontin. But she looked as sad as Hank.

For the rest of the week, we practiced for the grand finale. At the end of camp it would be us standing on the Outlook porch, playing for our parents, instead of the counselors playing for us. Ms. Rapontin was teaching us "The Star-Spangled Banner." Colonel Profundo was in meetings. Instead of musical chairs on the porch, we did extra sight-reading, where you don't know what song it is and try to play it just by looking at the music. We had lessons in the barn all week. Mrs. Saybrook was still in our classroom.

At least we still had canoeing and soccer. At breakfast, we ate cereal out of our cocoa mugs. At lunch and dinner, we drank milk out of them. Once, after dinner, we lined up and Hank put ice cream in each mug, all different flavors. "Might as well finish it up," he said. Even ice cream can be sad.

Suddenly, it was Friday. We had one last lesson with Ms. Rapontin. Then we had to pack our trunks. Hank sanded and filled the claw marks on the porch beams. By lunch, they were gleaming with new white paint. "For the parents," he said. "Some of them went here, so it's their last time, too."

Quiet time was an all-camp rehearsal in the soccer field. Cars started parking in the parking lot.

We almost didn't fit on the front porch of The Outlook, because it was the band and the orchestra together. First, the band played "The Bear Went over the Mountain." Then Damian played his solo from "Concerto Fabuloso." Then we all sang the Outlook song. Parents sang along.

Then the colonel said, "Thank you, parents, for sending us these fine musicians. If you have not heard already, it was an even more exciting summer than usual, thanks to General Blodgett's Regiment, the Shahboz brothers, and a bear. All in all, I prefer the Shahboz brothers. And now, Mrs. Saybrook, chairperson of the board of directors, has a few words to say."

"Oh!" said Mrs. Saybrook, and stood up. "Well, I just wanted to say, we have a positive though small bank balance this year. The porch is, as usual, about to fall off, and the bear damage didn't help. We had a very attractive offer from a developer for the property. In a special meeting of the board of directors, we have decided, however, to keep Outlook Music Camp going. Mr. Cyrus Shahboz has kindly donated all the royalties from his new composition, 'Concerto Fabuloso,' to the camp. It will be performed in London under the baton of his brother, Darius. One of the solos will be played by our own Damian Freewinkle. A CD will go on sale this Christmas. It would help if everyone bought several."

The parents all clapped. We stamped our feet and went "Woooo!" Hank turned bright red and hugged Mrs. Profundo.

"Freewinkle," said Byron.

"And now, before the porch falls off," said the colonel, "a song I dearly love."

We played "The Star-Spangled Banner." *Bup-pa, bwaaaah!* we finished, extra loud. A dog licked the back of my knee. It was Dante.

"Yayyy!" said Byron and I, and patted him.

"Yay? Is that all you promising beginners have to say?" said Damian, and patted him, too. Another hand was scratching Dante's ears, a hand with diamond rings and red nail polish. "I just love dogs," said Mrs. Saybrook.

Damian held out his hand. She shook it and said, "Oh, very nice playing, Mr. Freewinkle. But I really wanted to thank the promising beginners. I was always a promising beginner. In fact, all I ever played was 'Twinkle.' It was a great comfort to me to hear it the night the bear came. Although I am glad we still have a few of them around here. Bears, I mean. And promising beginners."

That was it. Dad came and took Dante's leash and scruffed my hair. Phoebe and Penelope both walked up to me. Phoebe fell down. I picked her up and she said, "Moo-gy," and clapped her hands.

"See?" said Mom. "She knows your name."

"Moo-gy," said Phoebe, again.

"Moogy!" said Byron. "Your new nickname for

hockey camp!" That was all I needed, my sisters *and* my best friend making fun of me. Plus, hockey camp. But I just played the happy running song with my mouth. Phoebe put her fingers on my lips and cackled. Penelope held on to my leg and blew a raspberry.

Look for these other books about Morgy:

Morgy Makes His Move

Texas Bluebonnet Award Master List
Children's Literature Choice List
Parents' Guide Award

★ "A superbly realized regional novel that is nonetheless universal: second- and third-grade readers from all over will enjoy watching Morgy make his move."
—*Horn Book,* starred review

"Lewis packs a lot of action into this short novel and plenty of changes into her hero's young life. . . . This lighthearted novel is filled with incident and warmth."
—*Kirkus Reviews*

"With the flair of Barbara Park but a relaxed spareness all her own, Lewis makes Morgy an entertaining standout who would be well worthy of a sequel."
—*The Bulletin*

Morgy Coast to Coast

"Lewis perfectly captures an active nine-year-old boy's life. . . . Supported by Chesworth's action-packed black-and-white drawings, Lewis keeps the hot pace going from beginning to end. . . . Bravo."

—*Kirkus Reviews*

"Morgy continues to be a great easy-reader friend for the uncertain and cocksure alike."

—*The Bulletin*

MT. LEBANON PUBLIC LIBRARY